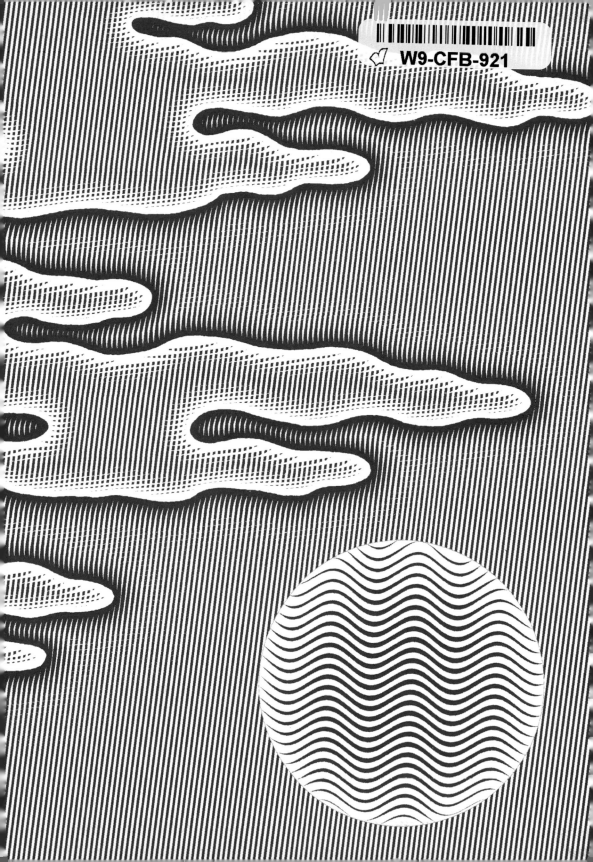

The Robber Chief

by W.W. Rowe

with visuals by Chris Banigan

Pandu «the Jeweler»

Mu «the Slave»

the Hermit

snow lion publications

ITHACA, NEW YORK ◆ BOULDER, COLORADO

snow lion publications

ITHACA, NEW YORK ◆ BOULDER, COLORADO

P.O.Box 6483, Ithaca, New York 14851
tel: 607-273-8519

ISBN 1-55939-087-5

Library of Congress Cataloging-in-Publication Data

Rowe, William Woodin.
    The Robber Chief / by W.W. Rowe; illustrated by Christopher Banigan.
        p.   cm.
        Summary: A tale of vengeance and compassion, demonstrating the law of karma.
    ISBN 1-55939-087-5
    [1. Fiction, Juvenile.]   I. Banigan, Christopher, ill.
    II. Title.
    PZ8. 1. R63700   2002
    398. 2'0951--dc21   97-401286
    [B]   CIP
                                                                           AC

Printed in Canada.

for Eleanor

CONTENTS

INTRODUCTION

In 1894, Paul Carus published a short novel entitled *Karma*. Leo Tolstoy praised it highly and retold the story in Russian. The following adaptation, The Robber Chief, should make the tale more accessible to young readers.

Tolstoy particularly liked the episode of the robber who tried to climb out of hell– demonstrating that the true happiness of any one person depends on the happiness of others. This episode strikingly resembles Grushenka's "onion" story (in *The Brothers Karamazov, 1881*) –a folktale Dostoevsky had heard from a peasant woman.

THE MIGHTY SLAVE

Pandu the jeweler scowled. "What is it, Mu? Why does the carriage stop?"

"The horses, master, won't behave."

Pandu snarled. He had important business in the town. "Well, find out why, slow-witted fool! I've seen more brains in donkey drool."

Mu, the giant slave, leaned forward, squinting. "Master! A body lies across the way. Maybe some robbers slit his throat ... Maybe they stole his money ... Maybe–"

"Don't just sit there, you fat toad!" Pandu clenched his fists. "Get out and clear the way!"

"Yes, master." Mu leaped down onto the road. He

was strong and obedient, but not exactly bright. "Wait, master! It's a homeless bum. He's on his feet now, see? He was just sleeping in the sun."

Pandu gnashed his teeth impatiently. He had such urgent business! "Mu, rough up that lazy dolt. I'll teach him to cause me harm!"

Mu's inky eyes gleamed excitedly. "Yes, master! I do!" He seized the man's arm and began to pummel him with a meaty fist.

The victim had curly, red hair. He didn't even try to resist.

"All right," growled Pandu. "That's enough. Let's get going."

The red-haired man uttered a long, low groan.

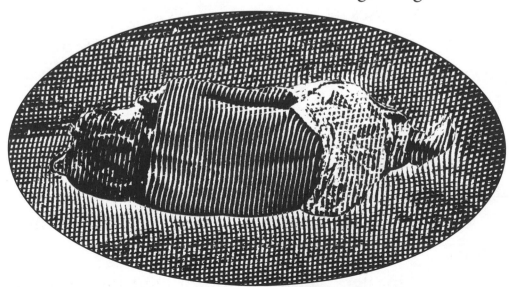

Mu leaped back onto the carriage, seized his whip, and lashed the horses. Once again, they rolled along the rocky road.

But soon the carriage slowed. They overtook an old monk, trudging toward the town.

Pandu sighed. "Mu, rough him up," he ordered. "No, wait. Stay there."

Long ago, Pandu had heard that if you help a holy man, it brings good luck. And so, forcing a kind smile, he said: "I am Pandu the jeweler. Would you like a ride?"

The monk nodded gratefully. He sat humbly by the jeweler's side. "I have no coins to pay," he said. "I'll give you Buddha's words instead." He began to murmur a prayer.

Mu grandly lashed the horses. The carriage rumbled on, bouncing and bumping. Then, once again, it stopped.

A farmer's cart had blocked the road. The man was hauling a huge load of rice.

The jeweler made a sour frown. He saw there was no room to pass. "You there!" he shouted. Move that cart, you brainless ass!"

"I can't, kind sir. This wheel is broke."

"Broke!? What is this? A conspiracy? I have important business. Mu, push that dung-heap into the ditch!"

"Yes, master." Mu leaped to the ground. A heaving, creaking sound followed. The cart collapsed, sliding into the deep ditch. The road was clear.

The farmer howled wildly. "I'll make you pay for that!" he shouted.

"If I were you," Pandu replied, brushing away a fly, "I'd stand politely to one side. "You saw what my mighty slave did to your cart. Now, he could tear you apart. Don't be a fool."

Mu's inky eyes lit up with hope. "This one is mine!" he thought.

What could the farmer do? He bit his tongue and stood aside.

But as the carriage began to roll, the monk held up his hand. "Excuse me if I leave you, sir. Perhaps we'll meet again in town. I wish to help this man because I recognize that he was one of your ancestors, in a prior life. So how could I repay you more than by helping him?"

"My . . . My ancestor?" Pandu spluttered. "Have you lost your mind!?"

"Excuse me, sir," the monk said softly. "This man, the one you have sorely offended, is tied to you invisibly—by karmic strands. I often find that shrewd men, to

such things, are blind. Your fate is closely intertwined with this poor farmer that you leave behind. You are acting, now, against yourself, but I will try to help."

"What drivel!" growled Pandu. "What foolishness! Your mind has rotted away, old monk. Mu, let's be off!"

The carriage sped away, but for the rest of his long ride, Pandu felt something deep inside, much like the aching of a tooth. He feared the old monk spoke the truth.

THE JEWELER'S PURSE

My cart is smashed!" the farmer moaned. "My rice is in the ditch! "I'll never get it to the market. That rat must pay for his foul crime!"

"Perhaps your cart can be repaired," the old monk said thoughtfully. He dragged two heavy pieces from the ditch.

The farmer blinked. "You're stronger than you look!" he said.

The old monk jumped and leaped about, pulling out the heavy pieces. He propped them up. He fit them tight. His blurry fingers flew back and forth.

The farmer stared, amazed. There seemed to be some wondrous, invisible force helping the monk. It was unbelievable! Soon his cart stood upright on the road. "You've even fixed the broken wheel!" he exclaimed.

"Glad to assist," said the monk. "But will you stand there saucer-eyed and watch me load these sacks of rice?"

The farmer's face went shameful red. "I'll do it too, of course," he said.

They both worked fast, and soon the cart was heaped with sacks of rice, ready to leave.

The farmer's horse was rested. The cart briskly, smoothly rolled along. The farmer said, "O holy man, you seem so wise. Perhaps you can explain why that man ill-treated me."

"For reasons that your eyes cannot detect," the monk replied. "In a past life, you may have betrayed him, or stolen his lovely wife, or caused him physical harm. So you must pay for your past deeds: you reap the harvest of those seeds." He smiled sadly. "Thus karma is with everyone. We are, right now, all we have done. And what we do to others now–always returns to us somehow." He gave the farmer a sharp look. "My friend, I read you like a book. You are hot-tempered, vengeful too–much like the man who injured you." He sighed. "You were not slow to duplicate the jewel-er's anger . . . and his hate. Besides, friend farmer, I suspect that in his place, you would have smashed the rice-cart too.

Come on, confess." He winked. "Or do I miss my guess?"

The farmer shrugged guiltily. "You're right," he said. "I must agree."

Suddenly, the cart-horse neighed.

"Look there! A snake!" the farmer cried.

The monk bent quickly down. In the roadside grass, he picked up a shiny, curved leather purse. "Oho!" he said. "This could be worse! It must belong to the jeweler, the man who did you wrong." He pried it open. "Ah, look! It's filled with gleaming gold! Just think. Fate offers you a treat! No revenge is half as sweet as doing good to those who have harmed you. Take this to town. Go to the inn and ask for Pandu. Give him his purse, and say that you forgive him. Say you wish him well. Because, friend farmer, I can tell that if he prospers, so will you. And if he's puzzled, tell him to come to the monastery, where I'll have some good advice to share."

III BUSINESS DEALS

The moon had risen when Pandu and Mu drove into town. Above the inn was a wooden sign showing a bed and a glass of wine.

"Unload!" the jeweler cried.

"Yes, master," said the huge slave.

Pandu quickly entered the tavern for a drink. There, at the bar, he caught sight of Balu the banker. "Balu, my friend!" He slapped him fondly on the back. "May all your gold, laid end to end, reach from this planet to the moon! May all your wives have children soon!"

"Pandu! May all your most expensive jewels be bought by rich and greedy fools!"

The two fat men embraced.

"Balu! My friend!"

"Pandu! My brother!"

Each man's wet lips left shiny streaks upon the puffy cheeks of the other.

But the banker looked sad. "Alas, Pandu! I have bad news. Regrettably, I cannot buy your jewelry now. You see, I made a business deal. But there's this man, my enemy . . . May fire ants infest his beard! May all his wives be sewer-smeared!"

"Keep calm, my friend!" exclaimed Pandu. "Who is this man? What did he do?"

"A rival banker," said Balu. "Somehow, he knew about my deal . . . May all his sons have leper's gout! May vultures pick his eyeballs out!"

"Calm down, my friend! What was your deal? What did this rival banker do?"

Balu let out a long, hissing sigh. "I made a contract to provide rice for the King. But that filthy swine, my enemy, has spies. Oh, that mangy hippopotamus! May both his ears leak stinking pus!"

"Yes, yes. That would be very nice. But tell me: What about the rice?"

"I just explained!" the banker cried. "I made a

contract to provide it. Tomorrow I must bring a cartload of the very best rice to the King. But that foul fiend (may he soon drown!) has bought up all the rice in town."

"Cheer up, Balu. He doesn't know we are friends. I'll go see him. Perhaps he will sell me a load of rice. I'll tempt him till he can't refuse. I've brought much gold with me. Here, take a look . . . Aiieee!" Pandu turned pale. He cursed loudly. He slapped his side. "It's gone!" he shouted. "That treacherous toad! He swiped my purse!"

Pandu glared wildly into space. He seemed insane with rage. "Help! Guards!" he cried. "Seize him!"

They searched both Mu and the carriage. They threatened the huge slave, but he denied everything.

They pulled a sack over his head. They flogged his back with the same whip he had used to lash the horses. They slashed and slashed.

"I'm innocent!" Mu groaned.

"Tell us!" they said grimly. "Tell us where you hid the purse!"

They shoved pins under his nails. They threatened him with branding irons.

"Confess, you rogue!" the jeweler cried.

"I'm innocent," groaned Mu.

Then, just as he was losing heart, the farmer arrived

with his load of rice. He gave Pandu the lost purse. "I forgive you for what you did," he said.

"But how?" cried Pandu, astonished. "But why?" He felt embarrassed and ashamed. "I wrecked your cart! You give me back my purse! It makes no sense. Have you gone mad?"

The farmer smiled and shook his head. "Go ask your friend the monk," he said. "He's at the monastery, where he has some good advice to share."

All this time, the tortured Mu was brooding angrily. Even when they set him free, he glared morosely at Pandu. He had a strange, vacant look in his eyes, like a dog about to turn on its owner. And that very night, he joined a band of reckless outlaws called The Fang.

The Fang lurked in the mountains, robbing any travelers who passed by. Mu proved to be such a savage fighter, they made him their new chief.

As for Balu, he gave a shout when he heard that the farmer had good rice to sell. "I'm saved!" he cried joyfully. "What good fortune!"

He paid the farmer double what he asked for his rice.

"I've seen the light!" the farmer thought. "I'm getting rich by doing right!" And then he gasped, because

Pandu also gave him a few gold pieces.

Burning with curiosity, the jeweler hurried off to see the monk. "What is happening?" he said. "I must admit, I'm mystified."

"I could explain," the monk replied. "But you would grasp it not. Instead, I'll give you some advice. Be sure your deeds are generous and pure. Sooner or later, all you do, both good and bad, returns to you. For karma never leaves your side–both now, and after you have died. Your selfishness must disappear. The path will then be true and clear."

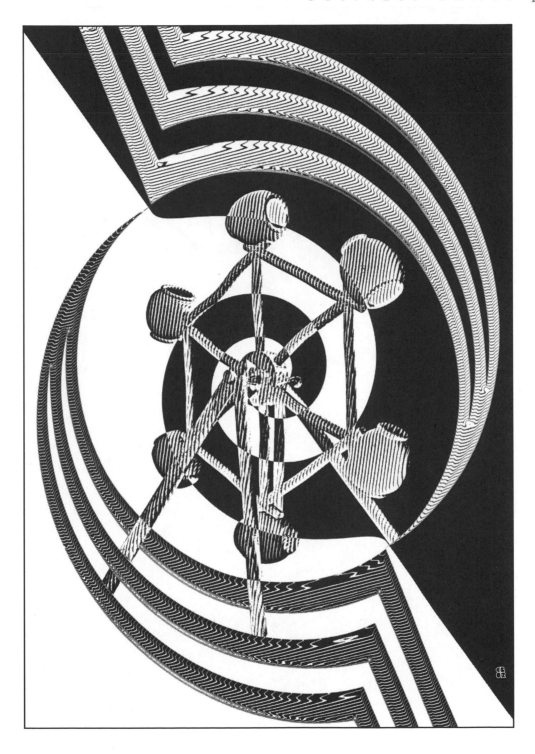

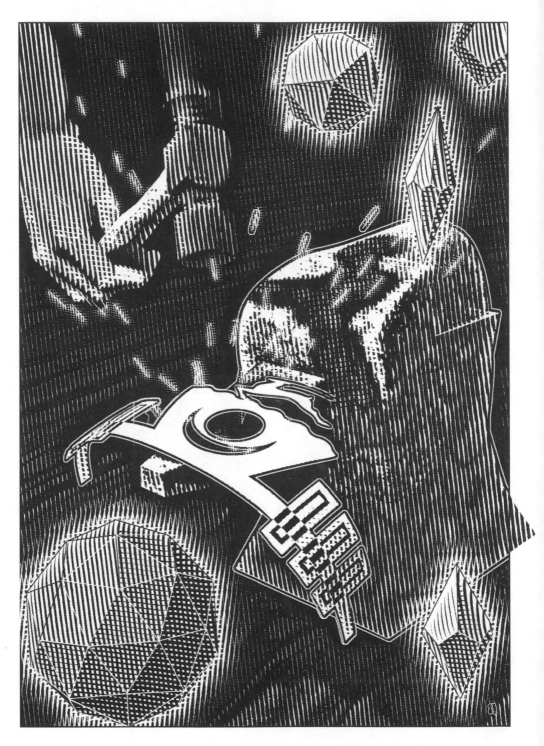

THE CROWN OF GOLD

The years passed by, and old Pandu made piles of money trading with Balu. But who could tell what karmic seed might ripen unexpectedly?

One morning, from another land, a messenger arrived, carrying an order from a famous King. The order was for a crown of gold, covered with precious gems!

Pandu was overjoyed. This would make him even richer! Very carefully, he crafted a gorgeous crown, inlaid with gleaming rubies, diamonds, pearls, and emeralds. The gold rose high in sweeps and swirls.

"This is my masterpiece," he thought. "He'll pay a fortune for it!"

With three armed guards, he left the town, clutching a large wooden box that held the crown. They rode through quiet, sunlit fields. The jeweler's head was filled with dreams of all the money he would receive.

The morning sun burned warm and bright. Not even a hint of danger. But then the stony road wound steeply upwards. Pandu's horse made a nervous leap.

Out from behind the rocks, a gang of thieves appeared. It was The Fang! Shouting wildly, robbers closed in from all sides. There was no way to escape.

On a big, white horse sat savage Mu. When he saw Pandu, his lips curled in a vicious smile. "Ah, master!

We meet again! What present have you brought for me?"
He snatched away the wooden box, and made a chop-like
signal to his men.

Three sword-blades flashed. Three round shapes
fell. Pandu let out a chilling yell.

Like three posts, his guards sat perched upon their
horses, but their heads rolled like three melons on the
ground. Their eyes still looked surprised and round.

"Don't kill me! Please!" Pandu begged.

"Of course not, master," Mu replied. "Beheading is
too good for you. You'll pray for death before we're
through." He rubbed his meaty hands together.

They tied the jeweler to a tree. They tortured him
in fiendish ways. His torments lasted for two days. On
the third, Mu roughly cried: "Well, master! Do you wish
you'd died? My men and me, we're getting bored. I'd fin-
ish you off, but that would be too easy. Instead, I've
saved the best for last."

He waved his hand, and from the crowd, a man
walked slowly forward. He had curly, red hair. "Remember
me?" he grimly said.

A long, low groan echoed in Pandu's bewildered
brain.

"We just found him yesterday," said Mu. He was

asleep, just like when you and I found him lying across the road. When you called me a fat toad. It's time he had his revenge."

Time passed. Just before sunset, a figure staggered toward the town. His fancy clothes were torn. A limp, broken arm dangled at each side of his body.

"The old monk was right," thought Pandu . "There's no escape, and I was caught. Sooner or later, all you do, both good and bad, returns to you. I caused others so much pain. How can I complain now?"

And then, he made a fervent vow. "I promise, always, to make sure my deeds are generous and pure." Pandu took comfort in this vow. It seemed to give him hope and strength. He felt a radiant, healing touch, although his arms still throbbed with pain.

He trudged slowly along, a faint, determined smile on his lips. Suddenly, he became conscious of a small shape, falling from above. It landed almost at his feet. He heard the faint cry of a baby bird.

Its feathers were blue. Its eyes were bright and pleading. When the little thing tried to fly, it let out a frightened, plaintive squeak.

Above his head, Pandu could see an empty nest on a low branch.

Still trying to fly, the bird made awkward little flips and flaps.

The jeweler sadly shook his head. "My wings are broken too," he said.

But then he saw a sight that made his blood run cold. On the ground, in a patch of shade, with lazy hostile glowing eyes, a long snake watched. It didn't move. It seemed to know that its victim could not escape.

Pandu's eyes widened desperately. He still had a sharp pain in each arm. But down he stooped. His fingers clasped the soft, frail bird. "Stay still," he whispered.

The nest was directly above his head. "I'll do this if it kills me," he thought.

Up, up he raised the baby bird. The pain became so great, his vision blurred. The tree branch and the nest turned grey.

But suddenly Pandu felt that warm, healing touch again. "There's something helping me," he guessed. And at last, his broken arm reached the nest.

The little bird was home. Pandu's heart filled with happiness.

Just then, the mother bird came swooping down from the sky. She landed quickly on the nest. She would protect her baby. Pandu was grinning. He felt blessed.

T R E A C H E R Y

V

Two years went by. Pandu gave all his jewelry profits to the monastery. "Now," he said, "your teachings can be widely spread. I only wish I could give more, like when I had that gorgeous crown."

His friend the monk smiled. "Your karma is being purified," he said. "It's hard to see right now, but your good deeds will help you in the future."

One day, a hermit made his way through the mountains. Suddenly, fierce Mu appeared with his bloodthirsty gang. "Stop, you fool!" he shouted. "We are The Fang!"

The hermit bowed respectfully. "And I . . . I'm poor, as you can see."

They searched the hermit from head to toe. Then they punched him a little and let him go.

Mu growled disappointedly. "We just wanted to make sure. Well, that'll teach you to be poor!"

The hermit limped away. He spent the night on some soft moss beneath a big tree.

The next morning, still stretched out on the ground, he was awakened by shouts and arguing. It sounded like a bitter quarrel. He heard the clashing of swords and a loud scream.

Jumping to his feet, he hurried through the woods and came upon a dreadful sight. The robbers, some quite bloody, were crowding in a circle, rushing forward, then drawing back.

And in the center, like a wild bear attacked by hounds, stood Mu, surrounded by his men.

They swung their flashing swords and knives, then sprang away to save their lives.

Each time, some of the robbers wounded Mu. Each time, he killed a man or two.

At last, he crashed down like a fallen tree.

The victors left. The rest had died. The hermit scanned them in horror. Only great Mu was breathing still.

The hermit propped up the giant's head. "I'll try to make you comfortable," he said softly.

Mu opened his inky eyes. "Where did those traitors go?" he snarled. "Ungrateful dogs! Vile cowards! I led them well! I gave them jewels!"

"Think not of that." The hermit sighed. "Your wounds are deep," he said.

"Wait! I remember you!" said Mu. "I beat you. I insulted you. And now, you are trying to save my life! Too late, good man. Those traitors have done me in. I taught them all! I showed them how to fight!"

"You should have taught them better things," said the hermit. "For each act brings its consequence. Do you know, now, where you are likely to go?"

"You're right! I'll roast in Hell!" cried Mu. "I'm doomed! There's nothing I can do!"

"That's never true," replied the hermit. "You can turn each moment into something new. Root out your hatred. Replace it with kind-heartedness. Before you die, try to care deeply about others. Listen now to the story I will tell you."

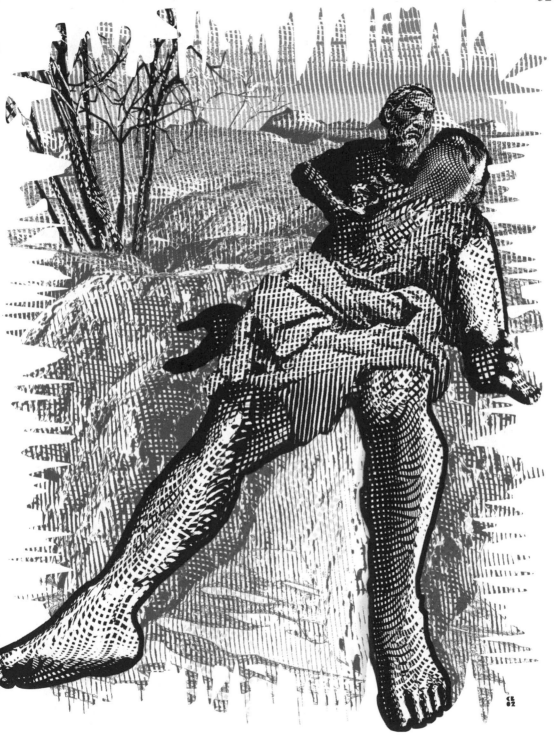

The Hermit's Story VI

On ancient times (the hermit began), there lived a savage, brutal robber chief. Kandata was his name. He did many terrible things, and died without remorse. But deep inside, Kandata knew that he would have to go to Hell.

And so he did. He was reborn as a green demon with an ugly horn, yellow claws, and frightened eyes. His body was a worse surprise. He had bright green, stretched-tight, tender skin, very delicate and very thin.

Each day, Kandata had to swim in flaming oil. From all around, tiny sharks came to gnaw his flesh. At night, he slept on nails and pins, while dreaming of his former

sins. Sometimes he had to walk in glades, where the grass was sharp, like little blades–and then would come the boiling rain!

Kandata's body writhed in pain. Each time his skin got burned and sore, it healed at once, ready for more. And so he lived for endless years, with endless agonies and fears.

But then the Buddha came to Earth. And when He attained Enlightenment, a dazzling ray of light pierced down to the deepest pits of Hell, shining with love and hope.

Kandata cried out mournfully: "O blessed Buddha! Pity me! I've suffered for so many years!"

The Buddha heard this from above, shining with selfless, radiant love.

"Kandata, did you ever do anything kind and pure and true? If so, it will return and help you rise anew."

Kandata squirmed in silence. Although he thought and thought, he was unable to recall doing anything kind! The robber's life had been filled with cruelty and sin.

But Buddha, the omniscient one, could see all the deeds of this man. He saw that once, Kandata found a spider crawling on the ground. And though he was

tempted to stamp out the creature with his shoe, he paused and thought: "I'll let him be. What has he ever done to me?"

So now, the Buddha smiled and said, "Here is a spider. See his thread? Take hold and pull yourself up from Hell."

Kandata, with a grateful shout, snatched at the web. Its thread was long and whispy thin–but very strong. It swayed and sagged, but didn't break.

Up, up Kandata climbed and swung! Above the flames of Hell he hung. At last, he gave a joyous yell:"I'm close! I'm close to climbing out!"

But suddenly he felt the thread stretch down. Five other sufferers in Hell were clinging to the web, also trying to climb out.

"Let go!" Kandata cried. "It's mine! The web is mine!"

With that, it broke. Kandata fell–and plummeted back into Hell.

THE SECRET CAVE VII

"What rotten luck!" said Mu. "I'm sorry for that demon-thief. Those other demons dragged him down."

The hermit shook his head. "That's not exactly it," he said.

"It's not?" said Mu. "Oh, now I know! He took too long. He climbed too slow."

"That's still not it." The hermit sighed. "Is it so hard for you to guess? Kandata still had selfishness. He was doing fine until he cried, 'This web is mine!' He should have thought about the others. Selfless love is like a light. It helps you to see what is right. And though the path is hard and long, by walking it, you make it strong. So helping others walk it too is really the best thing for you."

"Alas!" cried Mu. I know you're right. But I'm a gonner. Finished. Through. It's too late to help others. A thousand curses on my fate!"

The hermit regarded him closely. "Think hard," he said. "Perhaps you can do something."

Mu thought and thought. All of a sudden, his inky eyes grew bright. "I think I see," he said. "I feel better now. Let me tell you my story. I was a slave named Mu, owned by the jeweler Pandu. I left him when he tortured me–and I became the Chief you see.

"Two years ago, I got revenge. I robbed him too. I've heard he's now a holy man, helping others as he can. Please tell him I forgive him now. I hope he'll pardon me somehow. Please tell him that before I died, I also prayed for him–and tried to pay him back. Beyond that hill, there is a secret cave. It's hard to find. To open it, you press a tiny half-moon slit in the rock wall. Inside, I hid Pandu's gold crown. Inside that dark and secret cell, there lies a pyramid of precious gems. Please tell Pandu two others knew, but now they're dead, killed by old Mu. Tell him I hope he finds the cave. It's a . . . late present from his slave."

So saying, the robber chief drew his last breath. But at the moment of his death, his inky eyes shone wet and bright, like two stars on a misty night.

The hermit hurried into town and told Pandu about his crown.

The jeweler cried, "Ah, yes! Old Mu! It's good that he forgave me too."

Pandu took four strong men with sacks and weapons tied across their backs. On sleek brown horses, they sped directly to the place Mu had described.

But Pandu looked around, bewildered. "Rock walls are everywhere!" he said.

They searched all day, feeling each wall with their hands, but no half-moon slit did they find.

"Men," said Pandu, "that's enough. I fear there is no secret cave."

Turning to leave, Pandu caught sight of a blurry blue shape. It flashed and swooped. It seemed to fall. Its wings grazed one of the rock walls.

Then, awkwardly, as if in play, the blue bird quickly flew away. But near the spot its wings had hit, Pandu could see a small, curved slit.

His eyes grew wide. He cried: "That's it! The secret cave! The half-moon slit!"

But then he shuddered eerily and murmured, "Could it really be?" For in his mind, Pandu could see an empty nest in a low tree. And down below, he almost heard the faint cry of a baby bird.

His men were crowding all around. He pressed the slit. A grinding sound … The wall swung back … and they could see the treasure gleaming brilliantly. And right beside the gems, on the floor of the cave, they saw a magnificent gold crown!

Working fast, they filled the sacks. They were ready to go back. But first, at Pandu's command, they found the body of brave Mu–which, with full honor, they did burn and placed the ashes in an urn.

Then they returned to town. Pandu sold the jewels. He sold the crown. He helped the sick. He helped the poor. His deeds were generous and pure. He built a monastery too–tall, spacious, with a splendid view.

Inside, he placed the urn that held the ashes of Mu–with something added. Pandu the jeweler had carved some little birds upon its side, above these words:

Sooner or later, all you do,

both good and bad, returns to you.

Your selfishness must disappear.

The path will then be true and clear.

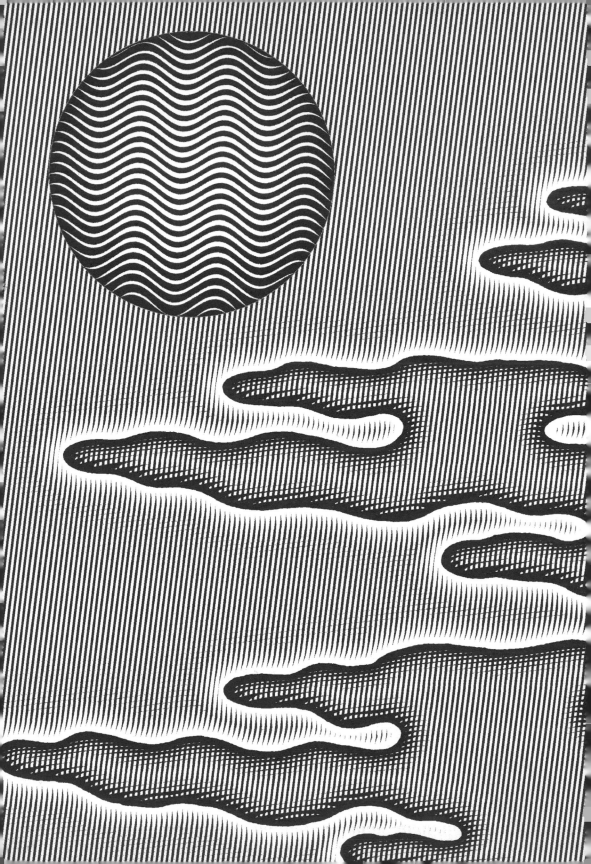